A Peddler's Dream

Janice Shefelman

Illustrated by Tom Shefelman

Houghton Mifflin Company
Boston   1992

To the memory of my father
Harold S. Shefelman
who also pursued his dream

T.S.

Text copyright © 1992 by Janice Shefelman
Illustrations copyright © 1992 by Tom Shefelman

Printed in the United States of America

Library of Congress Cataloging-in-Publication Data

Shefelman, Janice Jordan,
    A peddler's dream / Janice Shefelman ; illustrated by Tom
Shefelman.
        p.   cm.
    Summary: A Lebanese man who comes to the United States to seek his
fortune suffers several setbacks, but makes his dream come true.
    ISBN 0-395-60904-6
    [1. Lebanese Americans—Fiction.   2. Success—Fiction.]
I. Shefelman, Tom, ill. II. Title.
PZ7.S54115Pe   1992   91-35285
[E]—dc20   CIP
                            AC

BP   10   9   8   7   6   5   4   3   2   1

Solomon Joseph Azar lived in a small village in the mountains of Lebanon, but he had a big dream. He wanted to go to America and seek his fortune.

For a year he studied English at the American mission. Then in the spring he said farewell to his family and friends and Marie, his betrothed.

"When will you return?" asked her father.

"I'll come back for her as soon as I'm settled, *amm*."

"I'll be waiting," Marie said quietly.

For four weeks he sailed across the ocean. The ship was crowded with people who also had dreams. When the weather became rough, many of them had upset stomachs too.

But not Solomon. He stood at the rail and turned his face into the ocean breeze. After all, the blood of seafaring Phoenicians flowed in his veins.

The coast of America looked different from the snowcapped mountains of home. As far as one could see the land was flat.

And Solomon looked different from the people in the streets.

If I am to live in America, I will need American clothes, he thought.

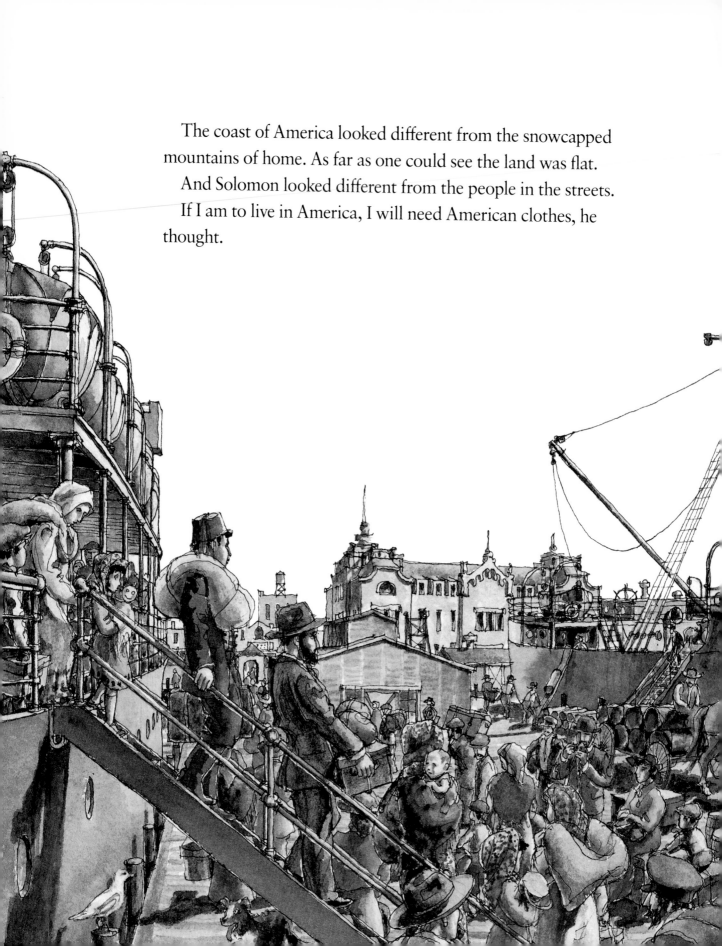

On Market Street he found a store that sold ready-to-wear for men and boys. He bought a new pair of trousers and a cap.

The owner was from the old country too, and Solomon asked if he needed a clerk.

"Sorry," he said, "I can't give you a job, but I'll give you some advice. The best way to get a start here is by peddling. Buy yourself a *quashaat*, a pack, fill it with things a farmer's wife needs, and off you go."

Solomon thanked him for the advice. He bought a pack and filled it with colorful calico, ribbon and thread to match, lace, suspenders, a few spices, and off he went.

He walked from farmhouse to farmhouse showing his wares. Calico sold for eight cents a yard and fancy lace for ten.

At the end of each day, if he was lucky, a farmer's wife would invite him to stay for supper and let him sleep in the barn. Then he would dream of having a real store and going back for Marie.

One cold rainy evening as he trudged through the hill country, two riders approached. They stopped, blocking his way.

"He's too small to be carrying such a big pack," said one. "Why don't we lighten his load?"

"Sure thing," said the other.

And they did.

When he awoke his head ached, his hands and feet were bound, and his pack was gone. So was his purse. Solomon had nothing left but his dream.

It was dark by the time he worked the knots loose. He picked himself up and started walking again. Though his body felt light without the pack, his heart was heavy.

Up ahead he saw the dim light of a farmhouse. Maybe they will let me sleep in the barn, he thought.

"*Wer ist er,* Papa?" asked a small boy in German. "Who is he?"

After Solomon told them who he was and what had happened,
Mr. Lindheimer invited him in. His wife gave him some dry clothes
and a blanket.

"I could sure use some help around the place, Solomon," said
Mr. Lindheimer. "I can't pay much, but at least you will have a roof
over your head *und* food in your stomach until you can think
what to do."

So Solomon stayed. He painted the barn and chopped enough wood to last for months. Sometimes while he cranked the cream separator, he entertained the little Lindheimers with tales from the old country.

All the while he dreamed of the store he would have one day. It kept getting bigger and bigger until it was four stories tall.

In the evenings after supper, Solomon often wrote letters home:

April 12, 1909

Greetings to the family of my betrothed:

I hope you are all well and the grape harvest was plentiful.

The hills here are not so high as our mountains, but the people are friendly and kind—at least most of them.

I look forward to the day when I can return and marry your beloved daughter. Please extend my greetings to her.

God's blessing on you,
Solomon

One day Mr. Lindheimer said, "I'm going to town tomorrow, Solomon. Why don't you come along? I'll introduce you to a friend of mine who has a dry goods store. It could be that he needs a clerk."

The next morning they hitched up the wagon and set off for Arcadia.

It was noontime when they came to the bustling town beside a river. As the wagon rattled across the bridge Solomon gazed up the broad avenue toward the state house. Streetcars clanged and people rode in horseless carriages.

"Well, what do you think, Solomon?" asked Mr. Lindheimer.
"I think this is the place for my store," he said.

Mr. Lindheimer pulled up in front of Hart's Dry Goods.
Solomon tied up the horses and followed him inside. The counters
were piled high with boxes, and the store was dark.

"Good day, Mr. Hart. This is my young friend, Solomon Joseph.
He peddled his wares across the state until he was beaten and
robbed near our place." He told how Solomon had worked hard
and learned fast, how he dreamed of having a store of his own
someday. "I thought he might be good help to you."

"Well, it happens I do need a clerk," said Mr. Hart. "Someone to
live in the apartment upstairs and watch over the place. Would that
suit you, my boy?"

It suited Solomon perfectly. For two years he worked in the store, sending money home as he was able. He persuaded Mr. Hart to install new light fixtures and ceiling fans. He cleared the counters so customers could see the rows of colorful ribbons, the fancy umbrellas, straw hats, and comb and brush sets. He always greeted them with a smile even when they wanted to return something. More and more people came to shop in Hart's Dry Goods.

Now that he was settled, the time had come to return for Marie. Happily Mr. Hart agreed, and Solomon sailed back to Lebanon.

On the wedding day his father led the horse carrying Marie through the streets to the church and Solomon. She was more beautiful than he remembered, especially in her headdress.

After days of feasting and dancing, Solomon and Marie returned to Arcadia.

Marie set about making their apartment into a home. She hung curtains in the windows and unrolled a colorful rug that was part of her dowry. The Harts gave the young couple a wing chair and a potted palm.

In the garden at the rear of the store Marie planted a fig seedling brought from the old country.

Before long a daughter was born to them, and they named her Rebecca.
Then came another, whom they called Ruth.

While Solomon worked in the store, Marie took care of the little girls.
In the afternoons she often invited friends over for sweet Arabic coffee,
and the children played in the garden.

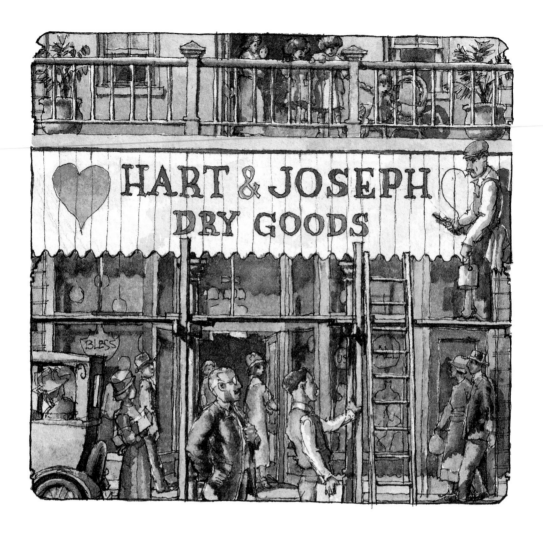

One day Mr. Hart said, "Solomon, you've brought new life to this old store. How would you like to be my partner?"

Solomon grinned. "Just what I had in mind."

So the store became Hart & Joseph Dry Goods. Although it was not the store of his dreams, it *was* a beginning.

Because Solomon made sure their store was always stocked with well-made items, business grew. Customers knew that shoes bought from Hart & Joseph would not come apart, that their cloth would not fade nor their underwear shrink.

Solomon's family grew too. When a son, Isaac, was born and
another daughter, Nora, he built a house on West Hill, close enough
to State House Avenue that he could walk to the store.

Now the store was called simply Joseph's, for Mr. Hart had retired to tend his cattle, sheep, and goats.

Solomon built a mezzanine for his office and remodeled the second floor to sell fine ladies' ready-to-wear from New York and Paris. The clothes were so stylish that the governor's wife came to shop when she needed a new dress for a party in the mansion.

"Only in America!" said Solomon.

Late one night the clanging of fire trucks awakened him. He jumped
from bed and looked out the window. A red glow filled the sky over
State House Avenue.

"The store! Marie, it's the store!" he cried.

"Oh, Solomon," she gasped. "It can't be."

Hurriedly he pulled on his trousers and ran out the door.

But it was the store. As Solomon stood watching it burn, Marie joined him, clutching Isaac and Nora by the hand. Rebecca and Ruth were right behind, their eyes big.

"Papa," cried Rebecca, with tears running down her cheeks, "it's ruined. Our nice store is all ruined."

Solomon put one arm around her shoulders, the other around Marie. "Yes, Rebecca, ruined but not finished."

Solomon was true to his word. He rented temporary quarters and purchased new merchandise. In two weeks he reopened for business with a fire sale on the sidewalk. Marie made *baklawa*, which they served to customers with coffee.

On New Year's Day Solomon resolved to build the store of his dreams. He bought property on State House Avenue at the corner of Hickory Street and hired an architect, Elijah E. Clayton.

"Make it four stories tall and make it the most beautiful building on the avenue," said Solomon.

So Elijah E. Clayton did.

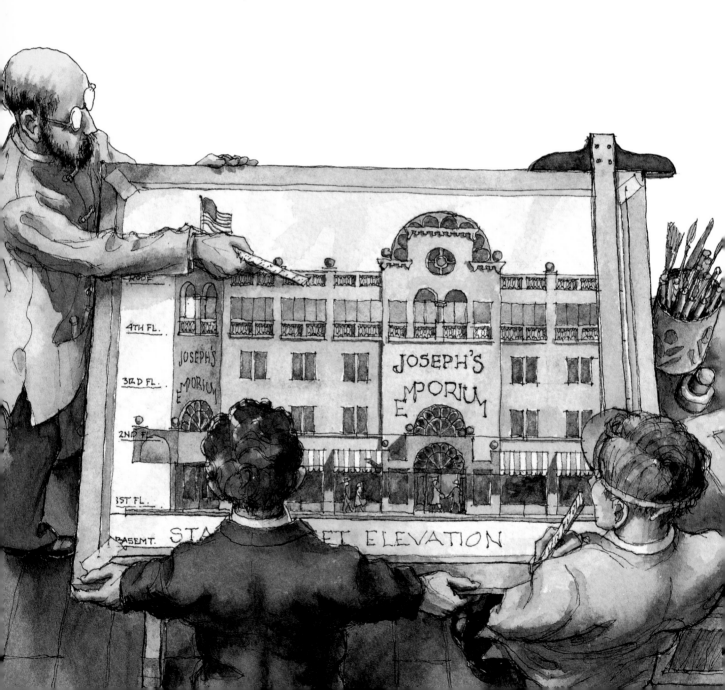

Each day Elijah came with his roll of drawings to make sure the store was built just as he had designed it. And Solomon came also—to make sure he made sure.

On opening night Solomon and Marie gave a party. The Harts came, the Lindheimers, and the governor too. When the musicians began to play, Solomon took Marie's hand and said, "*Habibati, my dear,* will you dance with an old peddler whose dream has come true?"

She smiled. "A peddler with a dream is *more* than a peddler," she said.

And they danced.